STORYWOODS

HANK HAS A DREAM

REBECCA DUDLEY

PETER PAUPER PRESS, INC.
White Plains, New York

Published by Peter Pauper Press, Inc.
202 Mamaroneck Avenue
White Plains, New York 10601
U.S.A.

Published in the United Kingdom and Europe by
Peter Pauper Press, Inc.
c/o White Pebble International
Unit 2, Plot 11 Terminus Rd.
Chichester, West Sussex PO19 8TX, UK

Designed by David Cole Wheeler

Library of Congress Cataloging-in-Publication Data

Dudley, Rebecca, 1963- author, illustrator.
Hank has a dream / Rebecca Dudley. -- First edition.
pages cm
Summary: Hank relates to a friend a dream in which he flies to the sea, past the trees, and over the clouds.
ISBN 978-1-4413-1572-4 (hardcover : alk. paper) [1. Flight--Fiction. 2. Dreams--Fiction.] I. Title.
PZ7.D86838Haq 2014
[E]--dc23

2014015662

ISBN 978-1-4413-1572-4
Manufactured for Peter Pauper Press, Inc.
Printed in Hong Kong

7 6 5 4 3 2 1

Visit us at www.peterpauper.com

Last night I dreamed I flew!

I was all by myself, but I wasn't scared.

I found a path, and I followed it . . .

. . . all the way to the sea.

As I went higher, I felt lighter and lighter.

I flew so far away.

Way out past the trees.

Then . . .   where was I?   Over the clouds!

And I flew faster than ever!

Then I came whooshing down!

But the last part was my favorite.

When I just . . . floated.

The whole dream?

Yes. Please.

Last night I dreamed we flew . . .

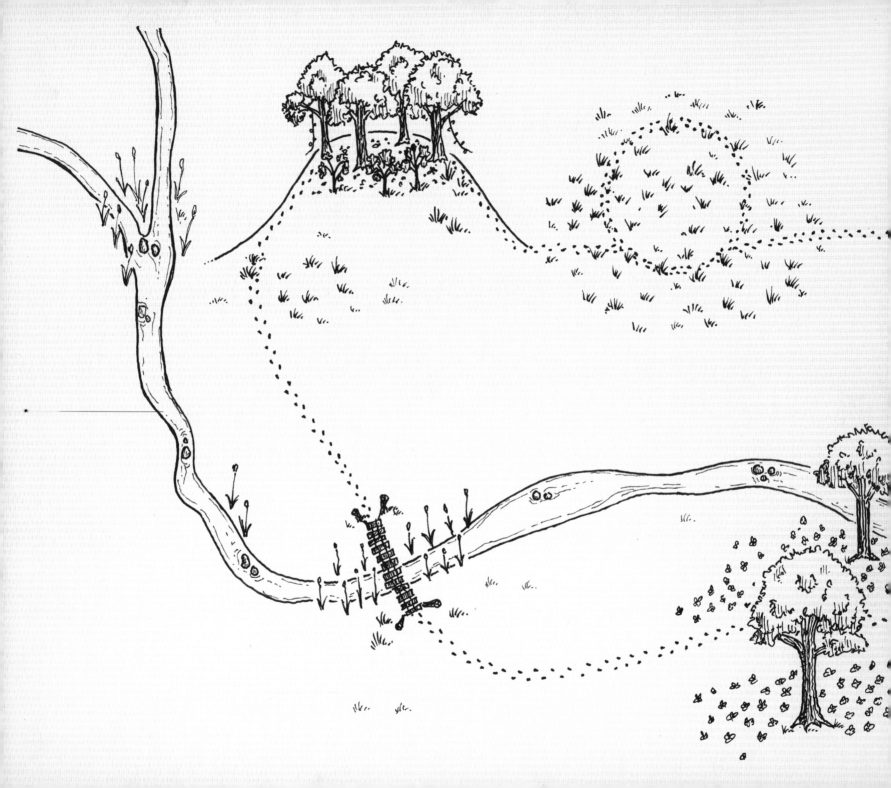